LITTLE MOUSE'S
VALENTINE

LITTLE MOUSE'S VALENTINE

DAVE ROSS

William Morrow and Company, Inc. • New York

Printed in the United States of America.

1 2 3 4 5 6 7 8 9 10

Library of Congress Cataloging-in-Publication Data

Ross, Dave, 1949–   Little mouse's Valentine.
Summary: Follows the adventure of Little Mouse as he goes to purchase a valentine.
[1. Mice—Fiction.   2. Valentine's Day—Fiction]
I. Title. PZ7.R71964Li   1986   [E]   85-15357
ISBN 0-688-06224-5   ISBN 0-688-06225-3 (lib. bdg.)

To Brian

Little Mouse wanted to buy
a valentine card.

"Be careful," cautioned Poppa Mouse.

"Hurry home," said Momma Mouse.

Little Mouse headed
for the door . . .

but the way was blocked.

"Oh, oh," thought Little Mouse.

Look out,
Little Mouse.

"Whew, that was close."

Little Mouse ran out
the door . . .

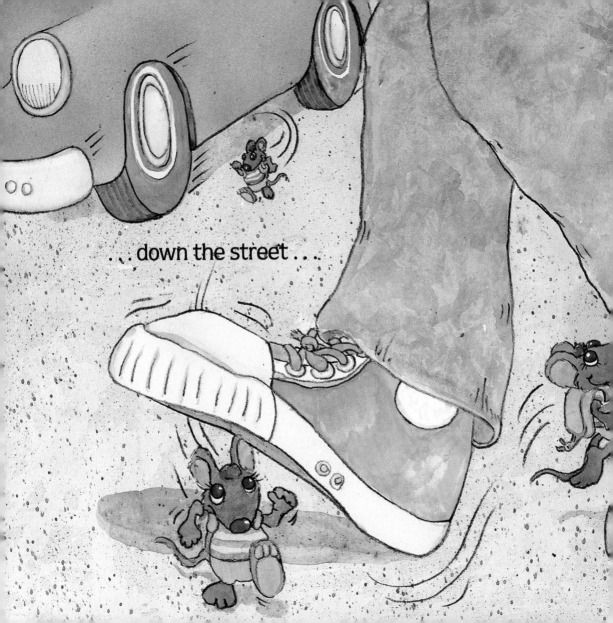

...down the street...

and into
the card shop.

Little Mouse looked and looked . . .

Little Mouse
left the
card shop . . .

and hurried home again.

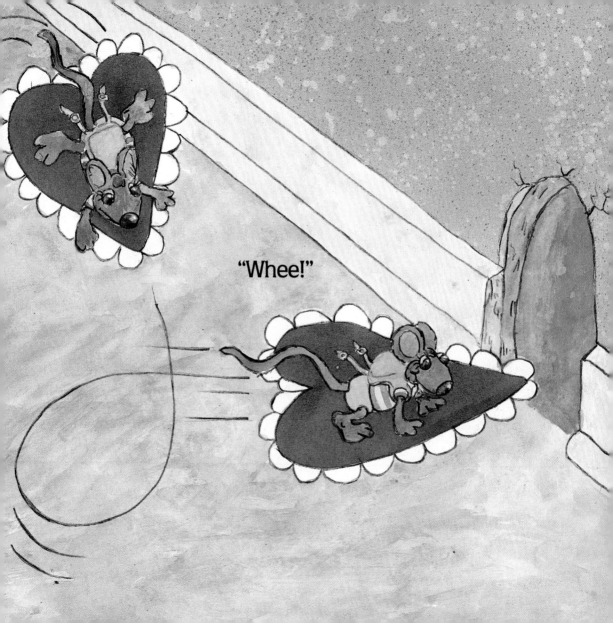

"Whee!"

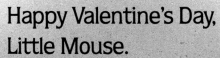

Happy Valentine's Day,
Little Mouse.